Caillou®

Goes Camping

Adaptation of the animated series: Roger Harvey
Illustrations taken from the animated series and adapted by Eric Sévigny

 houette

COOKIE
JAR

Caillou was playing
hide-and-seek with Grandpa.
He tiptoed into the living
room. "Where are you,
Grandpa?"
Caillou looked behind the
big chair. "Found you!"
Caillou laughed.

"Come on, you two. Snack's ready. We're waiting for you in the backyard."
Outside, Mommy had set the table for their snack. There were cookies, cake, fruit, and cold drinks on the table.
"We're coming, mommy."

"This reminds me of the first time I took your daddy camping when he was a little boy just like you," said Grandpa.
"Grandpa, why don't we go camping, just you and me?" Caillou asked.
"Great idea! And I think I know just the spot to go camping," said Grandpa.

Caillou and Grandpa set up the tent in the backyard. Caillou held one of the poles while Grandpa was busy inside the tent. Out of the corner of his eye, Caillou saw a squirrel and let go of the pole to chase the squirrel. The tent wobbled and then collapsed on top of Grandpa.

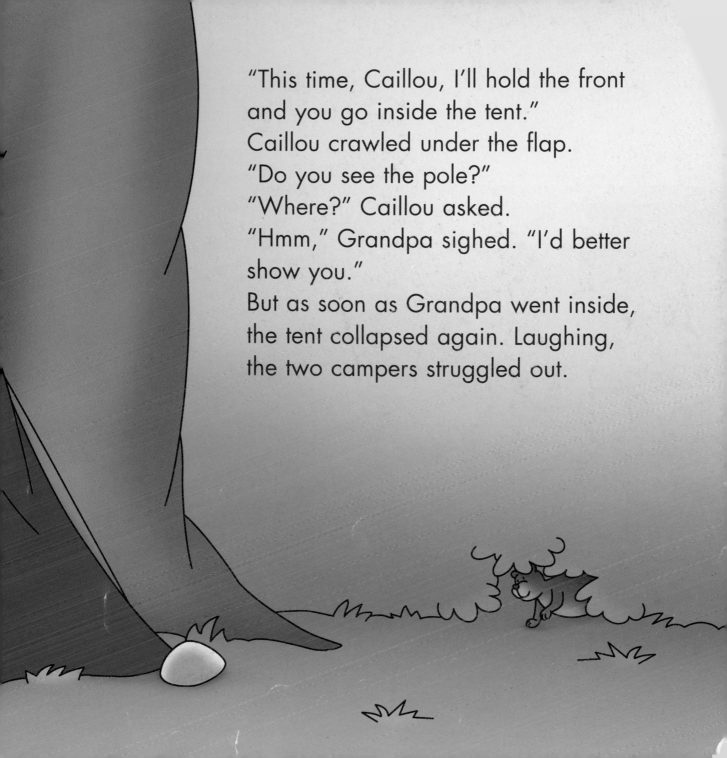

"This time, Caillou, I'll hold the front and you go inside the tent."
Caillou crawled under the flap.
"Do you see the pole?"
"Where?" Caillou asked.
"Hmm," Grandpa sighed. "I'd better show you."
But as soon as Grandpa went inside, the tent collapsed again. Laughing, the two campers struggled out.

Caillou heard the sound of birds chirping.
"Look, Grandpa, a bird's nest!" he said, pointing to a tree.
Grandpa picked Caillou up and lifted him to see the bird
feeding its young.
"Grandpa, there are two baby birds in the nest!" Caillou said
Grandpa put Caillou back down. "We'd better get our tent
up or we'll be spending the night under the stars."

Later that evening, Caillou and Grandpa sat roasting marshmallows over a small fire. "They look perfect!" said Grandpa, popping one into his mouth. "Mmm! Delicious!"

When it got dark, they wrapped themselves up in blankets and lay back admiring the starry sky. Grandpa started to yawn. "It's getting late. I'll get our sleeping bags ready," he said.

Caillou spotted some small lights flickering in the air.
"Grandpa, what are those lights over there in the bushes?"
"Those aren't lights, Caillou. They're fireflies."
Just then, a firefly landed right on Caillou's nose.

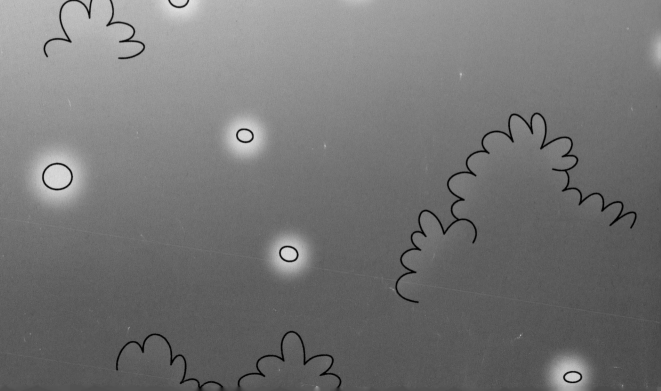

Caillou was stretched out in his sleeping bag. It was late, but he still couldn't get to sleep. Whoo! Whoo! Whoo! It was the hoot of an owl. Caillou opened his eyes and looked over at Grandpa, who was asleep beside him.

Caillou was getting scared, so he shook Grandpa to wake him up. Right away, Grandpa guessed what was wrong. He knew just what to do!

The next morning, a ray of sunlight shone into the tent.
Gilbert was curled up in a ball on Caillou's sleeping bag.
"What happened?" Mommy asked.
"Next time we go camping," said Grandpa,
"we'll ask that owl to be quiet!"

CAILLOU is a registered trademark of Chouette Publishing (1987) Inc.

Adaptation of text by Roger Harvey based on the scenario of the CAILLOU animated film series
produced by Cookie Jar Entertainment Inc. (© 1997 CINAR Productions (2004) Inc.,
a subsidiary of Cookie Jar Entertainment Inc.).
All rights reserved.
Original story written by Marie-France Landry.
Illustrations taken from the television series CAILLOU and adapted by Eric Sévigny.
Art Direction: Monique Dupras

The PBS KIDS logo is a registered mark of PBS and is used with permission.

We acknowledge the financial support of the Government of Canada through
the Canada Book Fund for our publishing activities.

Canadian   Patrimoine
Heritage   canadien

We acknowledge the support of the Ministry of Culture and Communications
of Quebec and SODEC for the publication and promotion of this book.
SODEC
Québec

Bibliothèque et Archives nationales du Québec and Library and Archives
Canada cataloguing in publication

Harvey, Roger, 1940-
Caillou goes camping
New ed.
(Clubhouse)
Translation of: Caillou fait du camping.
Originally issued in series: Backpack Collection. c2000.
For children aged 3 and up.

ISBN 978-2-89450-856-5

1. Camping - Juvenile literature. I. Sévigny, Éric. II. Title. III. Series:
Clubhouse.

GV191.7.H3513 2012   j796.54   C2011-942119-4

Printed in China
10 9 8 7 6 5 4 3 2 1 CHO1819 JAN2012